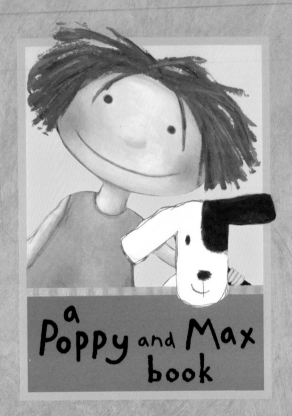

a **Poppy** and **Max** book

Time For Bed
Poppy and Max

Lindsey Gardiner

For Darcy -
who NEVER thinks it's time for bed!

little ORCHARD

ORCHARD BOOKS
96 Leonard Street, London EC2A 4XD
Orchard Books Australia
32/45-51 Huntley Street, Alexandria, NSW 2015
ISBN 1 84121 701 8 (hardback)
ISBN 1 84121 274 1 (paperback)
First published in Great Britain in 2002
First paperback publication in 2003
Text and illustrations © Lindsey Gardiner 2002
The right of Lindsey Gardiner to be identified as the author
and illustrator of this work has been asserted by her
in accordance with the Copyright, Designs and Patents Act, 1988.
A CIP catalogue record for this book is available from the British Library.
(hardback)10 9 8 7 6 5 4 3 2 1
(paperback)10 9 8 7 6 5 4 3 2 1
Printed in Singapore

This is
Poppy.

This is
Max.

It's time for bed but first Poppy...

drinks **one** glass of milk,

munches two biscuits and

gives Max three doggie treats.

1

2

3

4

Poppy washes **four** sticky paws.

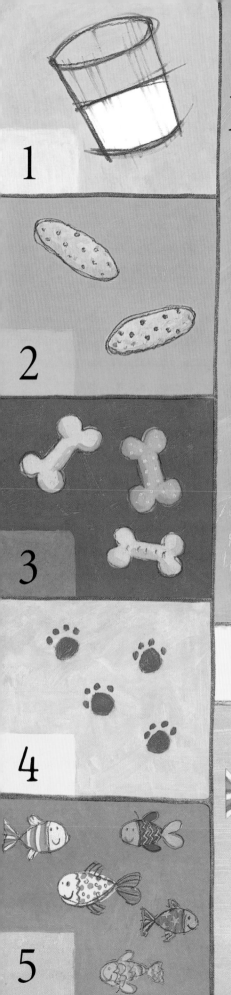

Max plays with **five** funky fish.

1

2

3

4

5

and Poppy blows **six** minty bubbles.

1

2

3

4

5

Poppy fastens
seven
pyjama buttons.

6

7

Poppy and Max read

eight picture books,

6

7

8

and cuddle up with nine toys.

Night, night, Poppy.
Night, night, Max.

6

7

8

9

Ten
twinkly stars
look down from above.

Sleep tight, Poppy.
Sleep tight, Max.

6

7

8

9

10

Bye
bye

See you again soon. . .